Moose and Mouse

Written By Mary Packard

Illustrated By Beth Weiner

LEVEL   READER

READING LEVEL
1
PRE K – GRADE 1

bendon®

This story's about
a moose and a mouse.

Moose and Mouse.
They share the same house.

Moose likes to *work*.

Mouse likes to *play*.

These two are different
in most every way.

Mouse is *messy*.
In fact, he's a slob!

Moose is *neat*
when he does a job.

Moose is **big**.
Mouse is *little*.

One plays the bass,
the other, the fiddle.

The bass is SO *large*,

and the fiddle so *small* . . .

. . . but Moose is not *short*
and Mouse is not *tall*.

In the morning at breakfast
they just can't agree.

Light toast or **dark**?
That's the problem, you see.

Should the cereal be *cold*?

Or should it be *hot*?

Whichever one chooses,
the other does not!

Moose and Mouse
enjoy driving about.

While one head is *in*,
the other is *out*!

There's never a problem
when they go to shop.

One picks from the **bottom**,
the other, the **top**.

They share the same bunk.

One *high* bed,

one *low*.

Mouse is *above*.

Moose is *below*.

One likes *less* light.

The other likes *more*.

But while they are sleeping . . .

. . . both Moose

and Mouse

snore.